T0198517

THE SONG OF ZONG

BY: WILLIAM A MOSES written & illustrated

To order additional copies of this book, contact:
Xlibris
844-714-8691
www.Xlibris.com
Orders@Xlibris.com

ISBN: Softcover   978-1-6641-3227-6
           EBook   978-1-6641-3305-1

Print information available on the last page

Rev. date: 10/01/2020

THE SONG

OF ZONG

Everyone, sing along;
sing the Song of Zong

Where everything is right
and nothing is ever wrong.

Even the sun would sing along
Here on the planet of Zong.

They once took a trip flew through Hong Kong.

**Wing Wing Wong,
Wing Wing Wong**

Hear the bells ring;

**Ding Ding Dong,
Ding Ding Dong**

Feel the bass drum thump;

Bing Bing Bong, Bing Bing Bong

Everyone, sing along; sing
the Song of Zong

Where everything is right
and nothing is ever wrong.

Even the sun would sing along,
Here on the planet of Zong

The choir sings along, Zongs sing the Song of Zong

Sing Sing Song, Sing Sing Song.

Here on the planet of Zong

Songs of Zong will help
you grow strong.

Sing Sing Strong, Sing Sing Strong.

Songs of Zong will help you livelong.

Ling Ling Long, Ling Ling Long.

You can climb tall buildings
just like Fling Flong

Fing Fing Fong, Fing Fing Fong,

Here on the planet of Zong

Everyone, sing along; sing
the Song of Zong

Where everything is right
and nothing is ever wrong.

Even the ocean would sing along
Here on the planet of Zong

Compete in Zong tournaments;
Play some ping-pong,

Ping Ping Pong, Ping Ping Pong

Every nightclub is singing;
come sing along!

Ting Ting Tong, Ting Ting Tong.

At Zongfest Zongs are singing;

Zing Zing Zong, Zing Zing Zong.

Everyone, sing along; sing the Song of Zong

Where everything is right and nothings is ever wrong

You can sing all day long (AND ALL NIGHT, TOO)

Here on the planet of Zong.

Printed in the United States
By Bookmasters